Mary-Anne
and the
Cat Baby

Pat Thomson

Illustrated by
Dee Shulman

OXFORD
UNIVERSITY PRESS

Great Clarendon Street, Oxford OX2 6DP

Oxford University Press is a department of the University of Oxford.
It furthers the University's objective of excellence in research, scholarship,
and education by publishing worldwide in

Oxford   New York

Auckland   Cape Town   Dar es Salaam   Hong Kong   Karachi
Kuala Lumpur   Madrid   Melbourne   Mexico City   Nairobi
New Delhi   Shanghai   Taipei   Toronto

With offices in

Argentina   Austria   Brazil   Chile   Czech Republic   France   Greece
Guatemala   Hungary   Italy   Japan   Poland   Portugal   Singapore
South Korea   Switzerland   Thailand   Turkey   Ukraine   Vietnam

Oxford is a registered trade mark of Oxford University Press
in the UK and in certain other countries

British Library Cataloguing in Publication Data

Data available

ISBN 978-0-19-915195-0

17 19 20 18 16

Mixed Pack (1 of 6 different titles): ISBN 978-0-19-915192-9
Class Pack (6 copies of 6 titles): ISBN 978-0-19-915191-2

Printed in China by Imago

Oxford OWL Discover eBooks, inspirational
resources, advice and support
www.oxfordowl.co.uk

Contents

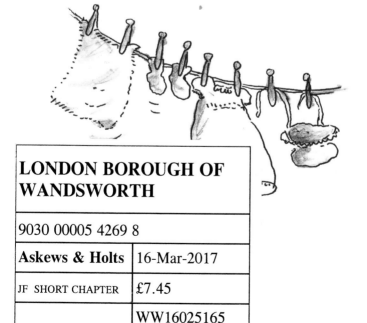

Chapter 1

Just for a Minute

Does your grandmother tell you that children were always good when she was young? Maybe, maybe not. That's all I'm saying – but read on.

This happened a long time ago when *my* grandmother was young.

I'm going to tell you about Mary-Anne.

She was a lively sort of girl. On Sundays she could look like a little angel. She wore coloured ribbons in her long, dark hair.

On other days, she lost her ribbons and her hair stood on end.

She wasn't an only child. She had three brothers and two little sisters. There was a big sister, too.

Oh! I nearly forgot the new baby.

So that was eight children.

No wonder their mother was always busy. This meant Mary-Anne often did things without asking her mother first.

If you promise not to copy her, I might just tell you about the time Mary-Anne got the cat mixed up with the new baby.

The new baby was very new. It slept a lot. It screamed a lot as well. To tell the truth, it was often quite smelly. Mary-Anne didn't like it much.

She also had a cat. That was quite new, too. The cat slept a lot as well. It never screamed and it was lovely and furry.

Mary-Anne thought Muffin the cat was much nicer than the baby.

One morning, there was just
Mary-Anne and her mother at home.
Mother was upstairs with the baby.

Mary-Anne was supposed to do the
potatoes for dinner but the sun was
shining.

It looked so nice outside. Perhaps
she could go into the yard first.
Just for a minute.

The big pram stood in the yard.
Prams in those days were like carriages
that horses pulled. They were high and
had bouncy springs.

Mary-Anne touched the pram. It bounced. She took the brake off and pushed it a little way.

Soon, she was parading up and down the yard, pushing the pram.

As she passed the gate for the third time, she heard a scuffling noise on the other side. An eye was looking at her through a knothole in the fence.

I know it's you, Josh Pembroke! You might as well come in!

The latch rattled and lifted and a boy came in. He wasn't like Mary-Anne. He was very tidy.

"You're not allowed to touch the pram," he said.

"It's supposed to be your tongue, silly," said Josh. "Can I have a push?"

Mary-Anne let him. After all, whatever it looked like, Josh *was* her best friend.

Josh took a turn with the pram. It was boring, pushing an empty pram.

"We need a baby," said Josh.

"Not ours," said Mary-Anne.

The baby's clothes were dancing on the washing line.

Mary-Anne looked at Muffin, then she looked at the little bonnet and lacy shawl.

Josh looked, too.

"I'll tell," he said but he took away the prop so Mary-Anne could reach the bonnet and shawl.

Mary-Anne wrapped Muffin in the shawl and laid him in the pram. Then she put his bonnet on and tied it carefully under his chin.

Muffin closed his eyes.

Mary-Anne and Josh
looked at each other.

"Open the gate," said Mary-Anne.
"Muffin needs to go for an airing. It's
good for him. All babies need to be
aired. Mother said so."

And they pushed the pram out into
the street.

Chapter 2

Airing the Baby

Mary-Anne and Josh paraded down the High Street, pretending to be grown-ups. They stopped and looked in the windows.

"Where shall we go?" asked Josh.

"Well," said Mary-Anne. "Mother always goes past the butcher's, past the greengrocer's and into the sweet shop."

"She never does!" replied Josh.
"She goes into all the other shops
and straight past the sweet shop."

They waved to the greengrocer.
He came out of his shop and stood
by the fruit and vegetables.

"Doing the shopping?" he asked.

"Yes," said Mary-Anne, "and airing
the baby."

"Helping your ma," nodded Mr Green. He smiled at someone behind them.

"Good morning, Mr Burton."

Mary-Anne and Josh looked at each other.

Mr Burton was Mary-Anne's Uncle Henry! He might know that Mary-Anne was not allowed to take the new baby out on her own. He might look in the pram.

Mr Green came over to them and put his hand on the pram handle.

"Here's two good little children," he said. "Your niece is helping her Ma to look after the baby."

"Is she now!" said Uncle Henry.

Both men bent over and looked in the pram.

"What the … ?" gasped Mr Green.

"Mary-Anne!" said Uncle Henry. "What have you been up to?"

Both men started to laugh.

"Your new nephew will have to start shaving quite soon. Look at those whiskers!"

"Good head of hair, too," said Uncle Henry. "Takes after me."

They laughed again and Uncle Henry gave them a penny each.

"Thank you, Uncle Henry," said Mary-Anne in a little, polite voice.

Mr Green picked out two apples and rubbed them on his apron.

"Here you are. Do call again."

"Thank you, Mr Green," they said.

They looked at each other. Then they both looked at the sweet shop.

They parked the pram and stood gazing in the window.

They took ages to choose. Sweets did not come in packets in those days. They were in big, glass jars.

Josh chose the humbugs in the
end and Mrs Munns weighed him out
a pennyworth into a little cone of
paper. Mary-Anne chose a big stick
of barley sugar.

As they left, Josh tripped over the step and nearly swallowed his humbug. Mary-Anne had to give him a big thump on his back.

They strolled away down the road. They were very happy.

Muffin snored gently in his pram outside the shop.

They had forgotten him!

Chapter 3

A Surprise for Mrs Belling

They did not talk much as they walked along. They were too busy sucking their sweets.

As they turned towards the park, a woman bustled towards them.

"Oh no!" cried Mary-Anne, "There's Mrs Belling. She'll want to see the baby."

"Don't worry," replied Josh calmly, "she never has her glasses."

"That's true," agreed Mary-Anne, but she still felt something was wrong.

Then she knew what it was.

Muffin! The pram!
We haven't got the pram!
We've left it outside the
sweet shop!

They both turned and ran back the
way they had come. Their boots
clattered on the pavement.

Outside the shop,
the pram was still
there, just as they
had left it. They
peered inside
and Muffin was
still asleep.

As they began to push the pram again, Mrs Belling came round the corner.

"My dears! How lovely. You're taking the new baby for a walk. What's the little angel's name? What does he weigh? Who does he look like?"

"His name is Muffin," said Josh.

"He hardly weighs anything," said Mary-Anne.

"He looks like his mother," said Josh.

"With bits of his father," said Mary-Anne.

Mrs Belling smiled. "You funny little things. I'll just peep. I won't wake him."

She leaned forward and looked under the hood.

She drew back. She looked again. Then she fumbled in her bag.

She had one last look in the pram.

Then she turned and hurried away up the street without saying goodbye.

"She didn't seem to mind," said Mary-Anne. "I hope she doesn't tell Mother."

They walked on to the park.

On the round bandstand,
men in uniform were playing
a march.

Mary-Anne and Josh stopped to
listen. They tapped their feet. They
waved their arms. It was no good,
they had to march.

This time, they did not forget
Muffin. Mary-Anne pushed him
round and round the bandstand
in time to the music.

They were enjoying themselves so
much, they didn't see someone watching.
A face peered out of the bushes.
It was a dirty face. They
didn't see him, but he
certainly saw them.

Chapter 4

Harry Meets Muffin

Mary-Anne and Josh were out of breath. They sat, puffing, on the grass.

A nursemaid came along, pushing a very shiny pram. An older boy walked by her side.

Mary-Anne called to the nursemaid, "Can you tell me the time, please?"

"Nearly midday," answered the nursemaid.

"Help! Mother will skin me!" yelped Mary-Anne.

The boy was peering into the pram.

"Never mind him," cried Mary-Anne. "I've got to hurry home."

They pushed the pram down the path which ran between the trees. They hurried as fast as they could.

Josh looked at the bushes beside the path. "Can you hear something?" he whispered.

Mary-Anne listened. "Yes. There's something in the trees."

rustle - rustle

"It's following us," said Josh in a very quiet voice. "I think it's a big animal. I heard it sniff."

"Wolves!" said Mary-Anne. "They can smell us. They'll hunt us down."

rustle rustle

Ouch! Drat!

"No, it's human!" yelled Josh. "Run!"

They flew down the path towards the
park gate. But the rustling and crashing
continued. It got faster, keeping up
with them.

Mary-Anne and Josh kept their hands
on the pram and their eyes on the gate.
Only a little further …

Then a dark shape shot out of the
bushes and stood in their path.

"Got you," it said.

IT'S
HORRIBLE
HARRY
BANKS!

It was the owner of the dirty face
which had been peering out of the
bushes at them. The rest wasn't too
clean, either.

Harry's hair was even worse than
Mary-Anne's. He had better things to do
than worry about his hair. On good
days, he looked like a hedgehog. On
bad days, his hair looked like the brush
they used to clean the school toilets.

"Go away, Harry Banks," said
Mary-Anne.

In fact Mary-Anne rather liked Harry.
He was more exciting to play with than
Josh.

"Don't have to," said Harry. "It's a
free country. What's in the pram?"

"It's the baby," said Mary-Anne.
Then she made a silly mistake.

She added, "but you can't look at it."

Now, Harry Banks was not very interested in babies. Until that moment, he had not even wanted to see the baby.

"I can look at it if I want to," he said. "Anyone can look at a baby."

"Just can't look at this one," said
Mary-Anne, very quickly. "This one is
different." Which was true, of course.

"How is it different?" asked Harry,
moving nearer.

Mary-Anne and Josh stood in front
of the pram.

"We'd like to show him to you but it might be a shock," said Mary-Anne.

"You might faint," added Josh. "We'll be going now."

Harry stood in the middle of the path, looking puzzled.

"I'll pay you," he said at last.

You can have my best marble.

Mary-Anne and Josh looked at each other. They smiled.

"All right," said Mary-Anne, "but be careful."

Harry handed over his marble. Then, very quietly, he crept up to the pram.

"Muffin *is* a baby," said Mary-Anne, setting off quickly towards the gate.

"Give me my marble back!"
Harry grabbed the pram handle.

Josh grabbed Harry's jumper. Harry
was yelling.

Some kind of rocket shot out of the
bushes. It was a barking rocket.

"Get 'em, boy," shouted Harry.

"It's only your Nip," said Mary-Anne.

Nip danced around, mad with
excitement. He smelled something.

With a leap, Nip was on the pram.

Muffin had been woken up by the noise. He saw Nip. He exploded out of the shawl and landed on the path. They saw him streak out of the park gates, still wearing the bonnet. Behind him raced Nip, barking happily.

Harry set off behind his dog.

Josh was still hanging on to Harry's jumper.

Last of all, Mary-Anne ran along as well as she could, pushing the pram.

Mary-Anne was really in trouble now!

Chapter 5

Stuck!

Mr Green was arranging the piles of apples in his window.

"My goodness! A cat in a hat! It must be Mary-Anne's kitten," he said, as Muffin flew past.

Then, "Josh and Harry in a hurry. What *is* going on? I must go out and see."

Sorry Mr. Green—

Muffin ran as fast as he could but he was only a kitten. He could still hear Nip behind him, panting hard.

In front of him was a tree. He leapt onto the trunk. He scrabbled with his claws.

The next moment, he was perched on a high branch, looking down on Nip.

Nip sat under
the tree and waited.
Harry and Josh arrived
next. They were out of breath
and cross with each other.
Mary-Anne and the pram arrived
last. She was out of breath, too.
She looked up.

Oh no! Muffin's right up the tree. We'll never reach him!

"Come to me, Muffin," cooed
Mary-Anne. "You're quite safe now."

Muffin stayed where he was.

Mrs Belling had finished her
shopping. She was with Mrs Whiting
and they both saw the children.

"There's something strange about the Burtons' new baby," she whispered to her friend.

"Is there, dear? Surely not."

Then Mrs Belling saw Muffin.

Aah! the baby's up a tree!

Mrs Whiting tried to calm her. "Don't be silly, dear. It's not a baby, it's a kitten. What happened?"

Mary-Anne explained about Nip, and Mrs Whiting took charge.

"Harry, Josh, can either of you climb that tree?"

"Easy, peasy," said Harry, and he started to climb.

As he climbed, Muffin scrambled higher up the tree.

"I can't get any higher," said Harry. His voice sounded a bit wobbly.

"Now we've got Harry *and* Muffin up the tree," sighed Josh.

"Mary-Anne," said Mrs Whiting,
"Run and fetch Mr Green. Tell
him to bring the shop steps."

Mr Green came running.
He put the steps under the tree.
He climbed to the top step and
stretched and swayed.

He still couldn't
reach either of them.

You could be in the ballet, Mr Green.

"Wait a minute," said Mrs Whiting. "The window cleaner does this street on a Tuesday. Run to the corner, Josh, and see if he's coming."

Josh returned with the window cleaner. He was carrying a very long ladder.

For some reason, he had a very big grin on his face. He set his ladder against the tree.

"Which shall I rescue first?" he asked. "The big creature or the pretty one?"

Mary-Anne began to feel better.

The window cleaner almost ran up
the ladder. He didn't mind the height at
all. He guided Harry safely down.

"I could have done it if I hadn't got
stuck," said Harry.

Mary-Anne felt sorry for him and
gave him a piece of barley sugar.

The window cleaner climbed again.

This time he stayed under Muffin,
making little cheeping noises and
speaking softly.

Soon, he gently put out his hand
and Muffin let him pick him up.
He buttoned the kitten into his jacket
and brought
him down.

Mary-Anne put Muffin back in the
pram and the three children, followed
by Nip, began to walk home.

Chapter 6

Just the Usual

It was rather a sad little procession.

Even Nip was quiet. Mary-Anne was worrying about what Mother would say. She still hadn't done the potatoes and it was so late.

Muffin, of course, slept on.

They turned out of the High Street into the narrow, cobbled lane.

When they reached Mary-Anne's gate, she opened it very quietly.

They crept in one by one, leaving
Nip outside.

The yard was empty. The back door
was still open but they could hear no
sound.

"Mother's gone out to look for me,"
gasped Mary-Anne. "Now I'm in
trouble."

"Go and check," said Josh.

Mary-Anne went indoors.

Josh took Muffin out of the pram
and put him to sleep in the sun.

Then he gave the shawl and bonnet
a good shake and pegged them
back on the line.

Mary-Anne
appeared in the
doorway looking
puzzled.

"They're asleep,"
she whispered. "Even
Mother! She's fast asleep."

"Get the dinner ready then," said
Harry. Under his hedgehog hair, he
had brains.

Very quietly, they peeled the
potatoes and put a pot of water to boil
on the big cooking range.

Mary-Anne was not allowed to put
coal in the stove, so Harry did it. Soon,
they felt the whole kitchen warming up.

They went outside again and stood
looking at each other.

"Clean the pram," said Harry.

Mary-Anne fetched a brush and
some dusters and they started to work
on the pram.

Suddenly, above their heads, a
window opened.

Mother was looking out of the
window.

Mother came hurrying into the yard.

"Oh dear," she said, "I'm all behind this morning. Baby was crying all night and we both just fell asleep."

Then she realised they were cleaning the pram.

"Just helping out, Mrs Burton," said Harry.

"The dinner!" gasped Mother.

"The potatoes are on, Mother," said Mary-Anne. It seemed best not to say anything else.

"Wonderful," said Mother. "I'll just heat the stew and there's some blackberry pie left. You must stay and eat.

Josh, run and ask your mother. Harry, what about you?"

"Ma's not in," said Harry, firmly. He liked stew and blackberry pie.

They sat round the big wooden table and tucked in. Their adventure had made them hungry but they were on their best behaviour.

"Now, what have you been doing today?" Mother asked.

"We went for a little walk," said Mary-Anne. "We met Mr Green."

"I hope you remembered your manners."

"Oh yes, Mother," said Mary-Anne.

"We met Mrs Belling, too. She asked about the baby."

"How kind. What about you, Harry?"

"Well Mrs Burton…" Harry was thinking quickly.

"Things are looking up," he said.

"That's excellent," said Mother, smiling. "So you all had lots to do."

"Not really," said Mary-Anne. "Just the usual."

It was true, you know. For Mary-Anne, that sort of day *was* usual.

About the author

My grandmother was born in Queen Victoria's time. She was always complaining about me and my brother and sisters. "You modern children!" she would say, shaking her head. "The way children behave these days!" Then she would tell us about what she used to do when she was little. I can tell you, we were angels compared with her.

This is one of her stories, and now I'm passing it on to you. I hope you enjoy it as much as we used to.